I want to GROW ↑

Ged Adamson

BOYDS MILLS PRESS
AN IMPRINT OF HIGHLIGHTS
Honesdale, Pennsylvania

For Helen

Boyds Mills Press
An Imprint of Highlights
815 Church Street
Honesdale, Pennsylvania 18431

Printed in China
ISBN: 978-1-62979-585-0
Library of Congress Control Number: 2016942355

First edition
Production by Sue Cole
The text of this book is set in Drawzing.
The illustrations are done in pencil, watercolor, and digital.

10 9 8 7 6 5 4 3 2 1

Herb **noticed** something about Muriel.

Something that became more obvious every day.

Muriel was getting taller.

And Herb didn't like it.

It wasn't that she could see things
he couldn't see . . .

or reach things he couldn't reach . . .

It was simply that he wasn't getting any taller himself.

"I need to find a way to catch up with Muriel," thought Herb.

The flowers gave
him an idea.

Herb planted himself
in the ground.
"Water me, Muriel,"
he said.

And he waited . . .

and waited . . .

and waited.

But Herb didn't grow at all.

Back inside,
Muriel was making things out of clay.
"Hmm. When you roll clay, it gets longer,"
thought Herb.

So Herb asked Muriel
to roll him.

She rolled him backward
and forward
until her arms ached.

But he didn't get any longer.
Just dizzy and a little queasy.

"I'll just have to force myself to grow," said Herb.

But it was no use.

Muriel thought she would cheer Herb up
with his favorite treat—tea and doughnuts.

But where was he?

"WOW! Herb, you look amazing!"

Herb's new outfit made him feel ten feet tall.
And, even better, it made him taller than Muriel.

But there was one problem
with Herb's new shoes.
It was almost impossible not to keep ...

falling over.

It had been a long day.
"I'll never grow," said Herb sadly.

In the morning, he went to wake Muriel.
"Good morning, Herb," said Muriel.
And then she noticed something.

As Herb jumped and cheered,
Muriel noticed something else.
She had grown, too!

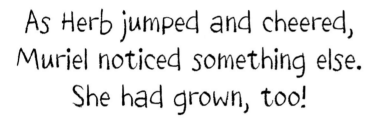

"What is it, Muriel?" asked Herb.
She thought for a moment.

"Nothing, Herb. Nothing at all.
Let's celebrate your new tallness!"

HOORAY!

So they did.
And Herb didn't worry about catching up
with Muriel because he was growing!